THE
COCK,
THE
MOUSE
AND THE
LITTLE RED HEN

RETOLD & ILLUSTRATED BY LORINDA BRYAN CAULEY

G.P. PUTNAM'S SONS   NEW YORK

Published simultaneously in
Canada by General Publishing Co. Limited, Toronto.
Printed in the United States of America.
Library of Congress Cataloging in Publication Data
Main entry under title:
The Cock, the mouse, and the little red hen.
Summary: A lazy cock and an equally lazy mouse
learn a lesson from an industrious hen who saves
them from becoming a fox's dinner.
[1. Folklore. 2. Animals—Fiction] I. Cauley, Lorinda Bryan.
PZ8.1.C643   1981   398.2′452   [E]   80-15666
ISBN 0-399-20740-6
ISBN 0-399-20930-1 pbk.
First Peppercorn paperback edition published in 1982.
First impression.

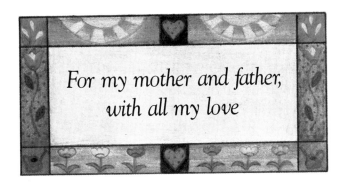

For my mother and father,
with all my love

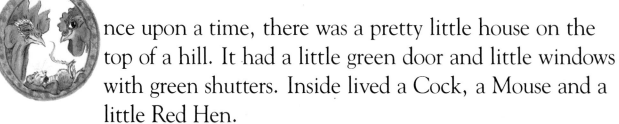 nce upon a time, there was a pretty little house on the top of a hill. It had a little green door and little windows with green shutters. Inside lived a Cock, a Mouse and a little Red Hen.

On another hill across the way, there was another little house. But it had a door that wouldn't shut, mostly broken windows, and all the paint was off the shutters. Inside that house lived a big bad Fox and four little fox kittens.

One morning, the little fox kittens said to the big bad fox, "Father, we are so hungry. We had nothing to eat yesterday, and only half a chicken the day before that."

The big bad Fox shook his head and then he said in a big rough voice, "On the hill across the way, I see a house, and in that house lives a Cock . . ." And before he could say another word, the little foxes all shouted, ". . . and a Mouse and a little Red Hen!"

"And they are nice and fat," went on the big bad Fox. "I will take my sack, cross the stream, go up the hill and in the door, and put the Cock, the Mouse and the little Red Hen into my sack and bring them home for supper."

The four little foxes jumped for joy and the big bad Fox went off to get his sack.

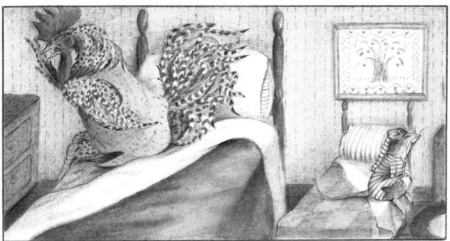

But what was happening to the Cock, the Mouse and the little Red Hen all of this time?

Well, the Cock and the Mouse got out on the wrong side of the bed that morning. The Cock said the day was too hot and the Mouse said the day was too cold. Grumbling all the way down the stairs, they went into the kitchen where the little Red Hen was already up and bustling about getting ready for breakfast.

"Who will get some sticks to make the fire?" she asked.

"Not I," said the Cock. "Not I," said the Mouse.

"Then I will do it myself," said the little Red Hen. And off she ran to get the sticks.

"Now who will fill the kettle from the spring?" she asked.

"Not I," said the Cock. "Not I," said the Mouse.

"Then I will do it myself," said the little Red Hen. And off she went to fill the kettle.

"Now who will get the breakfast ready?" she asked as she put the kettle on to boil.

"Not I," said the Cock. "Not I," said the Mouse.

"Then I will do it myself." said the little Red Hen.

All during breakfast the Cock and the Mouse quarreled and grumbled.

The Cock upset the milk jug and the Mouse dropped crumbs all over the floor.

"Who will clean up after breakfast?" asked the little Red Hen, hoping they would soon stop complaining.

"Not I," said the Cock. "Not I," said the Mouse.

"Then I will do it myself," said the little Red Hen.

So she cleaned up the dishes, swept up the crumbs, and brushed up the fireplace.

"Now who will help me make the beds?" she asked.
"Not I," said the Cock. "Not I," said the Mouse.
"Then I will do it myself," said the little Red Hen.
And she went upstairs by herself.

The lazy Cock and the grumbling Mouse settled
down in front of the fire and fell fast asleep.

Now the big bad Fox crept up the hill, into the
garden, and up to the window. If the Cock and the
Mouse had not been fast asleep they would have seen him
peeping in the window.

"Rat-a-tat-tat, rat-a-tat-tat." The Fox knocked on the
little green door.

"Now who can that be?" grumbled the Mouse, half-
opening his eyes.

"Go and see for yourself," said the lazy Cock.

"Maybe it's the postman with a letter for me," said the Mouse, as he went to the door. And without even looking to see who was knocking, he lifted the latch and opened the door.

And in walked the big bad Fox with a nasty smile on his face.

"Oh! Oh! Oh!" squeaked the Mouse and tried to run up the chimney.

"Doodle, doodle do," crowed the Cock and jumped onto the back of the chair.

But the Fox only laughed and popped them into his sack. And when the little Red Hen ran down the stairs to see what was happening, he popped her into the sack too. Then he took out a long piece of string and wound it round and round the sack so they couldn't get out.

The big bad Fox threw the sack over his back and started back down the hill. But the sun was hot and the sack was heavy and the Fox began to feel tired. He lay down under a tree for a rest in the shade and he soon fell fast asleep.

Snore, snore, snore. As soon as the little Red Hen heard the Fox sleeping, she took out her scissors and snipped a hole in the sack just big enough for Mouse to creep through.

"Quick," she whispered, "run as fast as you can and bring back a stone just as big as you are." Off ran the Mouse and soon came back dragging a stone just his size.

"Push it into the sack," said the little Red Hen.

Then the little Red Hen snipped away at the hole until it was large enough for the Cock to get out.

"Quick, she said, "run as fast as you can and bring back a stone just as big as you are." Off flew the Cock and he came back panting but with a stone just his size and pushed it into the sack.

Then the little Red Hen popped out and found a stone just as big as she was and she pushed it into the sack.

Then she put on her thimble, took out her needle and thread, and sewed up the hole.

As soon as she was finished, the Cock, the Mouse and the little Red Hen ran home, shut the door, fastened the latch, pulled down the shades, and felt safe again.

As the sun started to go down, the Fox felt cold and woke up. He sat up and rubbed his eyes. "Dear, dear," he said, "it must be late. I better hurry home."

The big bad Fox, grumbling and groaning, picked up the heavy sack and started out. But he had to cross the stream to get to the other hill. Splash! In went one foot. Splash! In went the other. But the stones in the sack were so heavy that Mr. Fox tumbled into a deep pool where the fish nibbled his toes and he dropped the sack altogether.

That night, the four little foxes had to go to bed once more without any supper.

But the Cock and the Mouse never grumbled again.
They fetched the water, filled the kettle, fixed the
breakfast, and made the beds while the little Red Hen
had a good rest sitting in front of the fire.

The big bad Fox never troubled them again and they are probably still living happily in the little house with the green door and the green shutters, on the top of the hill.